Did you See them too?

Neil Griffiths

Illustrated by Janette Louden

I thought I saw
an elephant,
sitting on
the stair.

Then I saw a python, hanging from the light.

But when I looked again, it had vanished out of sight.

And next
I saw a bear,
hugging
my TV.

But when I looked again, there was nothing I could see.

I even saw a monkey, swinging on the door.

But when I looked again, it wasn't there anymore.

Then I saw a lion, yawning on my bed.

But when I looked again, it was my teddy bear instead.

And yes I saw a penguin, washing in the sink.

But it had gone too, in the time it took to blink.

Is it only me, or did you see them too?

Are they really there,
or could it just be me?